Margaret Hillert's
Play Ball

A Beginning-to-Read Book

Illustrated by Oksana Kemarskaya

DEAR CAREGIVER,

The books in this Beginning-to-Read collection may look somewhat familiar in that the original versions could have been a part of your own early reading experiences. These carefully written texts feature common sight words to provide your child multiple exposures to the words appearing most frequently in written text. These new versions have been updated and the engaging illustrations are highly appealing to a contemporary audience of young readers.

Begin by reading the story to your child, followed by letting him or her read familiar words and soon your child will be able to read the story independently. At each step of the way, be sure to praise your reader's efforts to build his or her confidence as an independent reader. Discuss the pictures and encourage your child to make connections between the story and his or her own life. At the end of the story, you will find reading activities and a word list that will help your child practice and strengthen beginning reading skills. These activities, along with the comprehension questions are aligned to current standards, so reading efforts at home will directly support the instructional goals in the classroom.

Above all, the most important part of the reading experience is to have fun and enjoy it!

Shannon Cannon

Shannon Cannon,
Literacy Consultant

Norwood House Press • www.norwoodhousepress.com
Beginning-to-Read™ is a registered trademark of Norwood House Press.
Illustration and cover design copyright ©2017 by Norwood House Press. All Rights Reserved.

Authorized adapted reprint from the U.S. English language edition, entitled Play Ball by Margaret Hillert. Copyright © 2017 Margaret Hillert. Reprinted with permission. All rights reserved. Pearson and Play Ball are trademarks, in the US and/or other countries, of Pearson Education, Inc. or its affiliates. This publication is protected by copyright, and prior permission to re-use in any way in any format is required by both Norwood House Press and Pearson Education. This book is authorized in the United States for use in schools and public libraries.

Designer: Lindaanne Donohoe
Editorial Production: Lisa Walsh

LIBRARY OF CONGRESS CATALOGING-IN-PUBLICATION DATA
Names: Hillert, Margaret, author. I Kemarskaya, Oksana, illustrator.
Title: Play ball / by Margaret Hillert ; illustrated by Oksana Kemarskaya.
Description: Chicago, IL : Norwood House Press, [2016] I Series: A
    Beginning-to-Read book I Originally published in 1978 by Follett
    Publishing Company. I Summary: Because balls are used in many games and
    come in different sizes and shapes, when two young friends want to play
    ball they have trouble deciding which one to play with"-- Provided by
    publisher.
Identifiers: LCCN 2016001874 (print) I LCCN 2016022127 (ebook) I ISBN
    9781599538198 (library edition : alk. paper) I ISBN 9781603579902 (eBook)
Subjects: I CYAC: Balls (Sporting goods)--Fiction. I Play--Fiction.
Classification: LCC PZ7.H558 Pl 2016 (print) I LCC PZ7.H558 (ebook) I DDC
    [E]--dc23
LC record available at https://lccn.loc.gov/2016001874

288N—072016
Manufactured in the United States of America in North Mankato, Minnesota.

Do you want to play ball with me?
We can have fun.
I will run to my house and get a ball.

Now where is that ball?
Where did it go?
I have to find it.

Oh, here it is.
And here is something to go with it.
Now we can play ball.

Oh, no!
Look at you.
I guess we do not want this ball.

But I can get one that we will like.
I will run, run, run.
Do not go away.

No, no. Get down.
Dogs do not play this.
We do not want this ball.
It is not the one for us.

Here is the ball I want.
This one will work.
Here we go.

Oh, no!
What do I see now?
What do you have now?

We do not want this ball.
It is not the one for us.
What will we do?

Look, look.
I see something.
Is it a ball?

No, it is not a ball.
We can not play ball with it.
But it can go up.
See it go up.

Help, help!
Look at it go.
Away, away, away.

Oh, oh.
Down we come.
We do not like this.

Come to my house.
I have something that we can play with.
You will see.

Look at that.
I have a ball for that.
I will get it.

This ball is big.
It is fun to play with.
One, two, three.

And—
UP!

Now you do it.

Up, up, and in!
Oh, my.
This is fun.

Jump, jump.
Get it in!
This is the ball for us.

Now we can play ball.
Now we can have fun.

Foundational Skills

In addition to reading the numerous high-frequency words in the text, this book also supports the development of foundational skills.

Phonological Awareness: Phonograms —all, -ill, -ell

Oral Blending: Say the beginning sounds and word endings below for your child. Ask your child to say the new word made by blending the beginning and ending word parts together:

/b/ + all = ball	/f/ + all = fall	/m/ + all = mall
/h/ + hall = hall	/t/ + all = tall	/w/ + all = wall
/p/ + ill + pill	/h/ + ill = hill	/f/ + ill = fill
/w/ + ill = will	/b/ + ill = bill	/m/ + ill = mill
/s/ + ell = sell	/t/ + ell = tell	/f/ +ell = fell
/y/ + ell = yell	/d/ + ell = dell	/b/ + ell = bell
/sm/ + ell = smell	/gr/ + ill = grill	/sm/ + all = small
/ch/ + ill = chill	/sh/ + ell = shell	/st/ + all = stall

Phonics: Phonograms —all, -ill, -ell

1. Write the following phonograms (word endings) five times each in rows on a piece of paper: __all, __ill, __ell.
2. For each row, help your child write a letter (or letters) in the blank to make a word. If you have letter tiles, or magnetic letters, it may help your child to move the letter into the space.
3. Ask your child to read the rhyming words in each row.

Fluency: Shared Reading

1. Reread the story to your child at least two more times while your child tracks the print by running a finger under the words as they are read. Ask your child to read the words he or she knows with you.
2. Reread the story taking turns, alternating readers between sentences or pages of the story.

Language

The concepts, illustrations, and text help children develop language both explicitly and implicitly.

Vocabulary: Opposites

1. The story features the concepts of up and down. Discuss opposites and ask your child to name the opposites of the following:

run (walk)	here (there)	yes (no)	stand (sit)	hot (cold)
buy (sell)	sleep (wake)	over (under)	near (far)	outside (inside)

2. Write each of the words on separate pieces of paper. Mix the words up and ask your child to put the opposite pairs back together.

Reading Literature and Informational Text

To support comprehension, ask your child the following questions. The answers either come directly from the text or require inferences and discussion.

Key Ideas and Detail

- Ask your child to retell the sequence of events in the story.
- Why did they have so much trouble playing a game?

Craft and Structure

- Is this a book that tells a story or one that gives information? How do you know?
- Look at pages 28 and 29. How do you think the boys feel? Why?

Integration of Knowledge and Ideas

- What kind of balls do you like to play with?
- What game did the boys finally play together?

WORD LIST

Play Ball uses the 57 words listed below.

This list can be used to practice reading the words that appear in the text. You may wish to write the words on index cards and use them to help your child build automatic word recognition. Regular practice with these words will enhance your child's fluency in reading connected text.

a	find	jump	run	want
and	for			we
at	fun	like	see	what
away		look	something	where
	get			will
ball	go	me	that	with
big	guess	my	the	work
but			this	
	have	no	three	you
can	help	not	to	
come	here	now	two	
	house			
did		oh	up	
do	I	one	us	
dogs	in			
down	is	play		
	it			

ABOUT THE AUTHOR Margaret Hillert has helped millions of children all over the world learn to read independently. She was a first grade teacher for 34 years and during that time started writing books that her students could both gain confidence in reading and enjoy. She wrote well over 100 books for children just learning to read. As a child, she enjoyed writing poetry and continued her poetic writings as an adult for both children and adults.

Photograph by Glenna Washburn

ABOUT THE ILLUSTRATOR Originally from the Ukraine, Oksana Kemarskaya now lives in Canada. Drawing was her passion from an early age and her training has deep roots in Russian Fine Art. Oksana's work has appeared internationally in children's books, educational materials, and religious curriculum. www.kimazo.com